THIS BOOK BELONGS TO:

NAME: ....

AGE: ....

ADDRESS: ....
....

In memory of my Dad
- M.F.

To Orla
- R.M.

Text copyright © 2008 Mel Fisher
Illustrations copyright © 2008 Roisin Mathews

First published in Ireland by O'Donnell Press 2008
12 Coolemoyne Park, Jordanstown, Co. Antrim BT37 0RP
Telephone: 028 9096 6493
Email: b.odonnell93@ntlworld.com
www.odonnellpress.com

Special thanks to Roslyn, Matthew, Ben, Rachael and Dusty

A CIP catalogue record of this book is available from the British Library.

Printed in Ireland by GPS Colour Graphics Ltd.

ISBN 978-0-9553325-6-2

1 2 3 4 5 6 7 8 9 10

O'DONNELL PRESS

The Kingdom of
MOURNE

By Mel Fisher

Illustrated by Roisin Mathews

Right at the edge of the Kingdom of Mourne where the rugged mountains sweep down to the sea, Kiera sat on the rocks, moonlight glistening on her wings and her eyes stinging with tears. The rest of the clan always teased her about her wings; they made her feel like she didn't belong. Kiera's wings were brighter than all the other fairies; a golden sheen over her wings made her sparkle and glow with eye-catching brilliance. Tonight she'd had enough and after the first taunt she angrily flew down to the shore. No-one else was brave enough to leave the safety of the mountains, so here she was free from the endless teasing.

Kiera stared out at the moonlight shimmering its way across the sea into the cove. As she followed it she noticed that, hidden in the shadow of the rocks, there was a little boat bobbing on the water. She watched curiously as two burly men waded up onto the beach pulling the boat with them. Anchoring the boat securely in shallow water, they hauled a heavy bag out of the stern and dragged it along the stones to a small pony, waiting patiently at the top of the beach. The men heaved the bag up onto the pony and after carefully strapping it to the saddle, they began to walk briskly towards a stony path leading into the mountains.

Kiera leapt to her feet as she suddenly realised what was happening. "Smugglers!" she gasped. She knew exactly where they were headed, for the old Brandy Pad twisted its way through the mountains and was sometimes used by thieves and smugglers. Her heart pounded and her wings trembled; she knew she had to warn the rest of the clan.

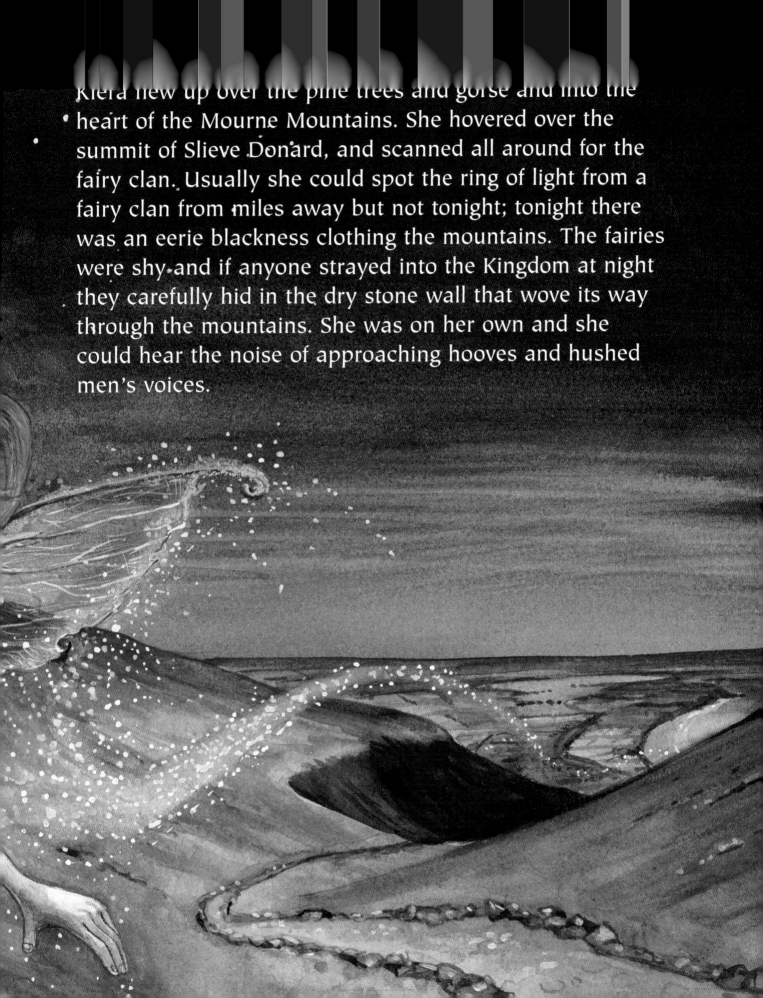

Kiera flew up over the pine trees and gorse and into the heart of the Mourne Mountains. She hovered over the summit of Slieve Donard, and scanned all around for the fairy clan. Usually she could spot the ring of light from a fairy clan from miles away but not tonight; tonight there was an eerie blackness clothing the mountains. The fairies were shy and if anyone strayed into the Kingdom at night they carefully hid in the dry stone wall that wove its way through the mountains. She was on her own and she could hear the noise of approaching hooves and hushed men's voices.

Calmly Kiera stretched her wings as high as she could and flew so that the moonlight reflected off her wings. She appeared as a flickering flame in the misty darkness and the pony quickly noticed her. Too frightened to continue, it stubbornly reared up. The heavy bag, strapped to the saddle, loosened and fell to the ground, gold and jewels spilling out over the grass. Angrily the men pulled at the pony's reins but it was no use; the pony refused to go any further. Determined to escape, the terrified pony broke free and bolted back along the path to the shore.

Leave it," said the taller of the two men.
"We'll have to carry the bag ourselves; we don't have any
time to lose. They'll be waiting for us at Trassey Track."
And with that he stooped to pick up the jewels and pack
them into the bag. He slung the bag over his back and
they trudged along the Brandy Pad, following the Mourne
Wall as it traced the outline of the mountains. Kiera sped
ahead and waited patiently at Hare's Gap.

Once she caught sight of the weary men she stretched her wings. Only this time she twisted into a spin forming the most stunning, dazzling light. The men stopped in their tracks, captivated by the golden shimmer. Then, as if in a trance, they followed Kiera deeper into the mountains.

Kiera, becoming weak from all the spinning, knew she needed the rest of the clan to try and stop the men. Desperate to find the fairies she put her fingers in her mouth and whistled. The high-pitched shrill echoed through the mountains and Kiera, now exhausted from her heroic efforts, spun out of control, crashing into the dry stone wall. She lay in a faded, crumpled heap, too tired to notice that hundreds of little lights were appearing from the spaces in the wall.

The tiny spinning lights glowed in the misty darkness and the men, terrified by the unexplained display of light, ran frantically along the mountain track. The uneven, stony path caused the men to stumble and fall down the steep slope. They rolled so fast they couldn't keep hold of the precious bag of jewels. Clinging to the grass and boulders, they managed to stop falling and sat terrified on a rocky ledge, as their bag continued to tumble down the mountain side. In disbelief they saw it reach the bottom of the slope and slowly sink into the boggy land just above the Silent Valley Reservoir.

Kiera lay motionless on the wall and the fairy clan gathered all around. Carefully Rosa the fairy chieftess drizzled sweet nectar from the yellow gorse onto Kiera's lips. As it dripped into her mouth a warm glow spread across her wings and she opened her eyes. "Oh Kiera, thank you for being so brave. Those golden wings made you very special tonight," whispered Rosa. Behind her Kiera could see the whole clan cheering in agreement. She smiled and sat up, proudly stretching her bright wings.

As the sun's rays began to stretch into the sky, the fairies spread along the wall and within seconds hundreds of fairies disappeared into the crevices between the stones. The golden-winged heroine was tucked away for a much needed rest.

The smugglers, stunned from their fall, gingerly stood up on the narrow ledge but there was no escape. They were surrounded by steep slopes and loose stones. A local farmer herding his sheep soon spotted the two men on the ledge above Silent Valley. A rescue was organised and the smugglers were quickly captured.

Despite a widespread search, the jewels were never found but on a misty black night visitors can sometimes see a flickering flame over the Silent Valley Park, where Kiera and her friends carefully guard the lost jewels.

THE KINGDOM of MOURNE

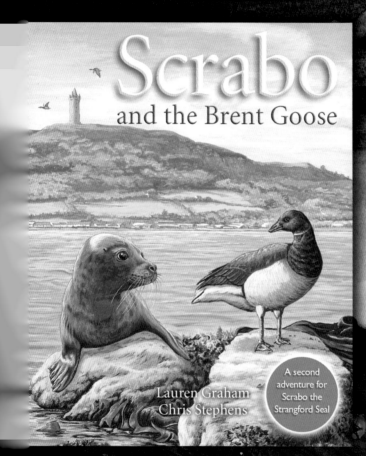
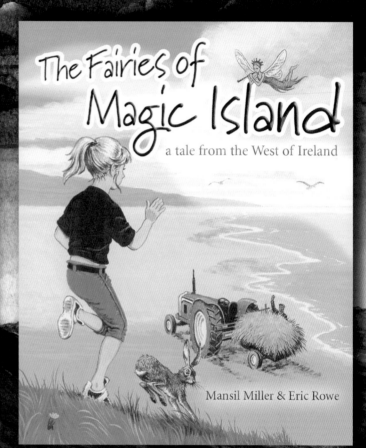